Little Rat
Sets Sail

MONIKA BANG-CAMPBELL

Illustrated by MOLLY BANG

HARCOURT, INC.

Orlando   Austin   New York   San Diego   Toronto   London

www.HarcourtBooks.com

First Harcourt paperback edition 2003

The Library of Congress Cataloging-in-Publication Data
Bang-Campbell, Monika.
Little Rat sets sail/Monika Bang-Campbell; illustrated by Molly Bang.
p.   cm.
Summary: With a little courage and a lot of practice, Little Rat overcomes her fear of sailing.
[1. Rats—Fiction. 2. Animals—Fiction. 3. Fear—Fiction. 4. Sailing—Fiction.]
I. Bang, Molly, ill.   II. Title.
PZ7.B2218Li   2002
[Fic]—dc21   2001001959
ISBN 0-15-216297-6
ISBN 0-15-204769-7 (pb)

E G H F D
A C E G H F D B (pb)

Manufactured in China

The illustrations in this book were done in pencil, gouache, and watercolor,
with some charcoal and chalk dust, on illustration board.
The display type was set in Elroy.
The text type was set in Adobe Garamond.
Color separations by Bright Arts Ltd., Hong Kong
Manufactured by South China Printing Company, Ltd., China
Production supervision by Sandra Grebenar and Wendi Taylor
Designed by Linda Lockowitz

With thanks to the Sea Education Association,
the Woods Hole Yacht Club, and the Quisset Yacht Club

To the memory of Buz, Tony, and Aaron

—M. B-C.

Chapter 1

Little Rat did not want
to take sailing lessons.
She was scared of the water.
She was scared of falling in.
She was scared of falling in
even with her life jacket on.
But Little Rat did not
have a choice about
sailing lessons.
Her parents just
signed her up.

On the first day of class,
Little Rat felt shy and nervous.
She looked different from everybody else.
Her life jacket was gray,
with a big red stripe across it
and laces up the sides.

Everybody else had on neat
yellow-and-orange zip-up life jackets.
Everybody else was cool.
Little Rat felt like a dork.
She wanted to go home.

To get to
the beach where
the boats were,
everybody had to go
down a long dirt hill.
Little Rat thought the hill
looked like a cliff.
How was she going to get down?
She could see only thin tree roots
to hang on to.
The other students ran down the hill,
whooping and hollering.
They thought it was fun.

Little Rat was
scared she would
fall and hurt herself.
She was embarrassed
the others would think
she was a fraidy cat.
Little Rat WAS a fraidy cat.
She went last so nobody
would look at her.
She went very, very slowly.

Buzzy Bear, the head instructor,
was waiting at the beach.
He showed the students the two kinds
of boats they would be sailing.
The javelins were floating in the water,
tied to moorings.
Little Rat thought they didn't look so bad.

Then Buzzy Bear pointed to some very
small boats sitting on the beach.
"Those are prams," he told the class.
"Only one person can fit in a pram.
You get to sail them by yourself."
Buzzy Bear said this like it was
a good thing.
Little Rat thought the prams were too tiny.
They looked like bathtubs
with masts sticking out of them,
and how could a bathtub possibly float?

Little Rat looked out at the water.
It was deep, dark ocean water.
She knew it had jellyfish in it,
and slimy eels,
and big icky blobs of seaweed.
Little Rat did not want
to sail a pram
by herself
in that water.
She did not want to sail at all!
She hunched down.
Maybe if nobody saw her,
they would forget she was there.

Chapter 2

Buzzy Bear told a story about
the first time he had raced a pram.
"I climbed in and sailed it
to the starting line," he said.
"I sailed back and forth
and waited for the race to start."
Buzzy Bear smiled.
"I was very big, even when
I was little," he said.
"And while I was waiting,
my pram filled up with water.
No race for Buzzy Bear!"
Buzzy Bear and the other students
laughed and laughed.

Little Rat did not think the story
was funny at all.
She stared at her little brown toes.
Tears ran down her face into her whiskers.
Buzzy Bear walked over to Little Rat
and gave her a hug.
"How about coming with me in a javelin,
Little Rat?" he asked.
He rounded up three other students,
and they motored out to the boat.
Little Rat stopped crying.
She was relieved she would not
have to sit alone
        in a sinking bathtub
            in the middle of an ocean
            full of jellyfish and slimy eels.

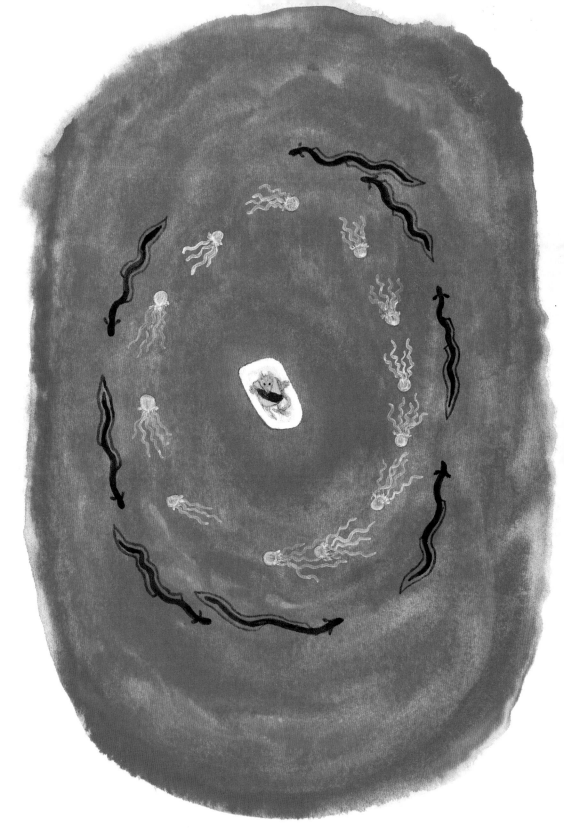

Buzzy Bear showed the students how to
put up the sails and sail off the mooring.
Little Rat thought, *This isn't so bad.*
The boat began to lean to one side.
Little Rat screamed, and scrambled
to the high side of the boat.

She was sure it was going to tip over
and they would all fall into the water.
"Don't worry," said Buzzy Bear.
"This is called heeling.
The boat won't capsize."

"What is *capsize*?" asked Little Rat.
She was suspicious of that word.
Buzzy Bear said, "*Capsize* is when the boat
tips all the way over and floats on its side."
This answer did not comfort Little Rat.

Buzzy Bear showed them how to make
the boat stop heeling by letting out the sails.
That made Little Rat feel much better.
She felt better for the rest of the afternoon.
Buzzy Bear made her feel safe.

Chapter 3

The next week, a new student
named Agnes came to class.
Buzzy Bear took her out
in a boat with Little Rat.
Just after they had sailed off
the mooring, the wind swept them
onto a sandbar.
Agnes hung on to the side of the boat
and wailed at the top of her lungs.
"We're sinking! We're going to die!"
she cried.

Little Rat was happy they were stuck
in the sand.
They could not capsize in the sand.
"Why are you crying, Agnes?" she asked.
"We're not sinking. We're not even
moving!"
"But we're stuck!" Agnes wailed.
Buzzy Bear hopped out of the boat and
began to push it off the sandbar.

Little Rat wanted to help.
She wanted Agnes to stop wailing.
But Little Rat did not want
to get into the water,
because crabs might bite her toes.
The water was very shallow.
It only came up to Buzzy Bear's knees.
Little Rat took a deep breath
and jumped in beside Buzzy Bear!

But the water came up past *her* belly button.
Not so shallow for Little Rat!
Back into the boat she climbed.

Little Rat stood next to Agnes.
"How can I help from *inside* the boat?"
Little Rat asked.
"Pull up the centerboard," said Buzzy Bear.

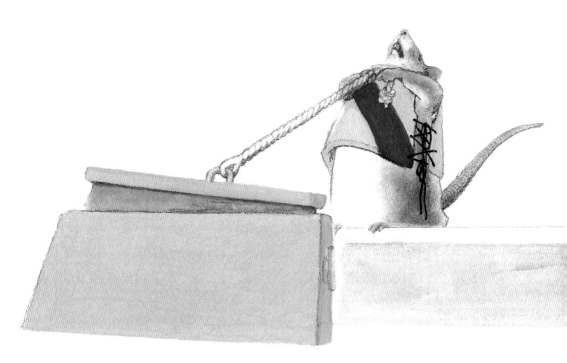

Little Rat pulled the centerboard rope.
The centerboard popped up out of the sand.
They were floating again!

Buzzy Bear pushed them into deeper water
and climbed back in.
He and Little Rat were all salty and wet.
Little Rat held the tiller as the boat
sailed forward.
The breeze dried her off.
The salt left white powder all over her fur.

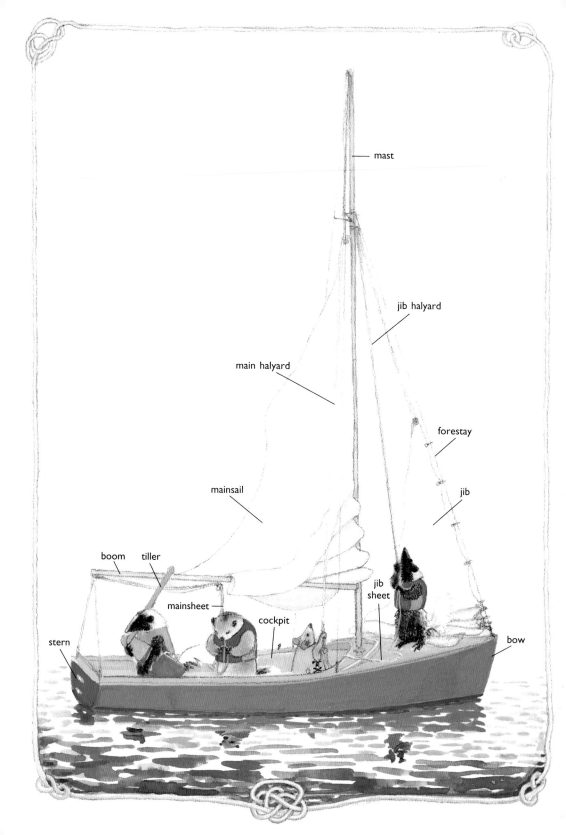

mast

jib halyard

main halyard

forestay

mainsail

jib

boom

tiller

jib sheet

mainsheet

cockpit

stern

bow

Chapter 4

Little Rat went to sailing class
every day, even though she was
still afraid of the water.
She felt sort of safe inside the boat.
She began to learn the different lines
and how they made the sails work.
Different lines were for different sails.
Little Rat liked to put up the mainsail.
She could raise the mainsail
from inside the cockpit.
But she had never put up the jib.
To clip on the jib, she would have to
step out onto the bow of the boat.
There was no protective railing
around the bow of the boat.
One misstep, and Little Rat would fall
into the deep, dark sea.

One day,
all the other
students in the boat
put up the mainsail.
Putting up the jib
was the only job left.
Little Rat had to do it.

She picked up the jib.
She wriggled out
onto the bow
on her bum.
If she stayed on her bum,
she could not
fall overboard.
But she couldn't
clip on the jib
without standing up.

Very carefully, Little Rat stood.
The boat was rocking.
Her little legs were shaking.
Clip by clip, she attached the jib
to the forestay.
Then Little Rat scooted back
into the boat.
Her heart was racing.
It was scary out on the bow.
But she had done it!
The jib flopped back and forth
in the breeze.
The boat was ready to sail.

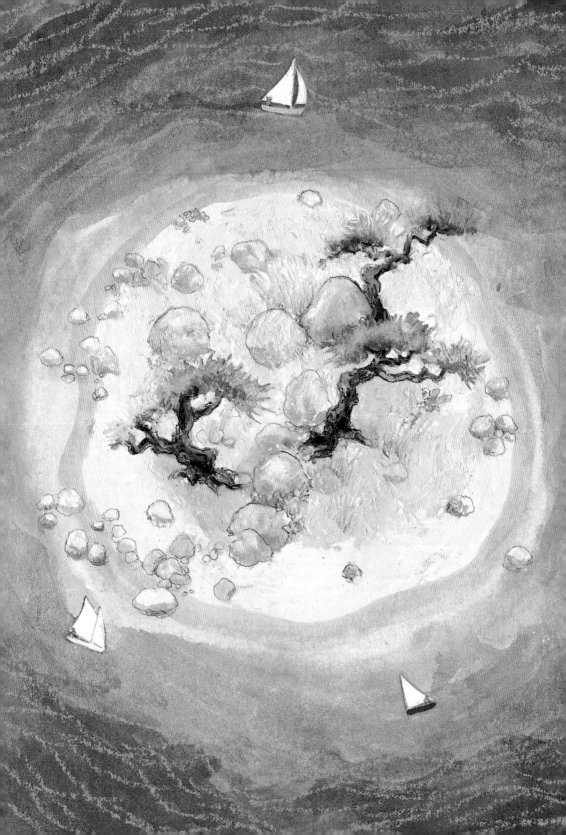

Chapter 5

All summer long, Little Rat
went to sailing lessons.
Then, on the very last day,
the class went on a picnic
to Blue Heron Island.
Blue Heron Island was
a pile of rocks and sand
on the other side
of the harbor.

The sun was shining.
The sky was blue.
There was a slight breeze,
but not enough to make the boats heel.
Little Rat sat in the javelin with her
friends and looked behind her.

All the boats were sailing in a line.
We are a parade, she thought.
We are a parade of boats.
Little Rat put her salty, wrinkled feet
up on the seat.
"This is a good day," she said to herself.

When they got to the island,
everybody jumped out and pulled their
boats up onto the beach.
Little Rat and her friends ate a picnic
lunch and played in the sand.
Then everybody went swimming.

Almost everybody went swimming.
Little Rat built a sand castle.
She strolled along the beach and
picked up jingle shells.
She lay on her towel and looked up
at the sky.
It was getting cloudy.
The clouds were getting bigger.
They were getting darker.

Buzzy Bear looked up
at the darkening sky, too.
"Time to head back.
It looks like rain," he said.
Everybody scrambled out of the water.
They packed up their stuff.
They pushed the boats off from the beach
and raised the sails.

And THEN...
there was no wind.
Sails do not work without wind.
They just sit and flap in the air.
The clouds grew bigger and bigger
and moved closer and closer.
The boats were going nowhere.

"I have an idea," said Buzzy Bear.
"We'll tie all the boats together in a line.
I'll tow you back with the motorboat."
So the students tied the boats together,
bow to stern.
Buzzy towed them to the harbor.
Just as they got back, the rain poured down.
Everybody moved fast to moor the boats
and furl the sails.

Little Rat's fur was soaked,
but she didn't care.
She had made it to the last day
of sailing lessons!
Her mama was waiting
at the dock.

When they got home,
her mama gave her a hot bath
and dried her off with a big fluffy towel.
Little Rat sat on the couch
while her mama rubbed her feet.
"Little Rat, you had lots of adventures
this summer," said Mama Rat.

"You went down
a scary steep hill
every day."
"It got less scary
the more I did it,"
said Little Rat.

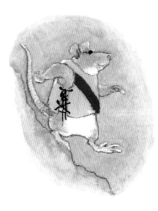

"You got stuck on
a sandbar and
jumped into the water,"
said Mama Rat.
"Not doing *that* again,"
said Little Rat.

"You put the jib up
all by yourself,"
said her mama.
"That was scary,"
said Little Rat.
"Yes," said Mama Rat,
"and you were brave."